This book belongs to:

_____

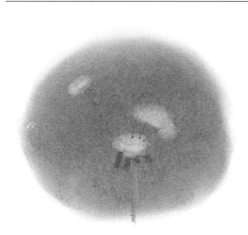

For Emma

Forever our happy shining sunflower

Love Mum and Dad

This paperback edition published in 2012 by Andersen Press Ltd.

Published in Australia by Random House Australia Pty., Level 3, 100 Pacific Highway, North Sydney, NSW 2060.

First published in Great Britain in 2010 by Andersen Press Ltd.

Text copyright © Jeanne Willis, 2006

Illustration copyright © Tony Ross, 2006

The rights of Jeanne Willis and Tony Ross to be identified as the author and illustrator of this

work have been asserted by them in accordance with the Copyright, Designs and Patents Act, 1988.

All rights reserved. Colour separated in Switzerland by Photolitho AG, Zürich.

Printed and bound in Singapore by Tien Wah Press.

Tony Ross has used watercolour in this book.

10   9   8   7   6   5   4   3   2   1

British Library Cataloguing in Publication Data available.

ISBN 978 1 84270 606 0

This book has been printed on acid-free paper

Mayfly Day

Jeanne Willis   Tony Ross

ANDERSEN PRESS

Here is Mayfly.
It is her first day on earth.
It is also her last.

Mayflies only live for one day.
But is she sad? Not at all.
She is happy to be alive!

This isn't any old day.
This is the *best* of days.
She lives for each moment.

She sees the world begin.
She hears the crack of dawn.
And bathes in its golden glow.

A billion buds burst open.
All for her!
She tastes their honey.

Mayfly sees eggs hatch.
Babies born.
Lambs learning to stand.

The business of ants.
The dizziness of children…
The loveliness of things.

She feels the sun's warm hug.

The kiss of summer rain.

The magic of the rainbow.

It is her wedding day.
Trees throw confetti.
There are games on the lawn.

Breezes blow, bells chime.
Birds sing! She dances
to the music of the universe.

Mayfly lays her eggs.
It is a peaceful night.
The *best* of nights.

She makes one last wish:
"Little ones, may all your tomorrows
be as perfect as my yesterday!"

Mayfly watches the moon come up
and the stars go out.
And is thankful for her wonderful life.

Other books by Jeanne Willis and Tony Ross:

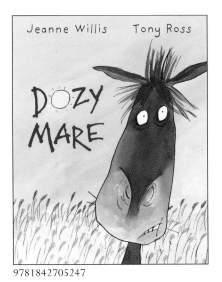

9781842705247

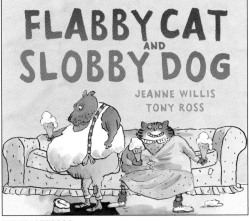

9781842709825

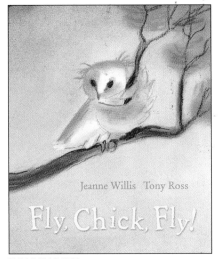

9781849394383

9781842709450

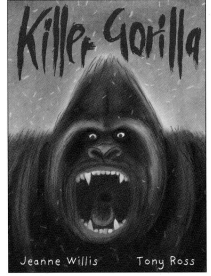

9781842705544

9781842707111